Book Club Edition

WALT DISNEY'S

DUMBO
the Flying Elephant

Random House **New York**

First American Edition

Copyright © 1978 by Walt Disney Productions. All rights reserved under International and Pan-American Copyright Conventions. Published in the United States by Random House, Inc., New York, and simultaneously in Canada by Random House of Canada Limited, Toronto. Originally published in Denmark as DUMBO–DEN FLYVENDE ELEFANT by Gutenberghus Bladene, Copenhagen. ISBN: 0-394-84093-3   ISBN: 0-394-94093-8 (library bdg.)

Manufactured in the United States of America 1 2 3 4 5 6 7 8 9 0 A B C D E F G H I J K

The circus had come to town.

All the circus people were getting ready
for the show.

While the ringmaster gave orders,
the workmen put up the last big tent.

The circus animals were busy, too.

The mother leopard licked her new cub.

The mother camel was proud of her new baby.

And the mother seal was happy her baby had come.

But one animal was not happy.
Mrs. Jumbo, the elephant,
had been waiting a long time for her baby.
But so far it had not arrived.

Then one day
the little elephant was born.
All the elephants came to admire him.
"He's so sweet!" said the proud mother.
"I wonder what I should name him."

Suddenly
the baby sneezed.
AH-AH-CHOOOOO!
And his ears flew up
in the air.

All the other elephants
laughed when they saw
how big his ears were.
"How funny he looks."
"I'd call him Dumbo."
"He looks like a Dumbo!"

And Dumbo was the name that stuck!
But Mrs. Jumbo loved her new baby.
"To me you are the most beautiful
elephant in the circus," she told him.
"I know you will be a star someday."

The next day the circus paraded
through town.

A band played as the elephants marched
in a line.

Dumbo was the smallest so he was
at the end of the line.

One child pointed at Dumbo's big ears.
But the little elephant didn't mind.
He was happy to be part of the parade.

Then suddenly
Dumbo stumbled.

First he stepped
on his right ear.

Then he stepped
on his left ear.

And finally
he fell flat
on his face.

All the children laughed.
Dumbo was very sad.

"You will never be a circus star
that way," one of the elephants told him.

Then a boy shouted,
"What a clumsy elephant!"
This made Dumbo's mother
very angry.
She picked up the boy
with her trunk and shook him.
"Help! Help!" he screamed.

"Oh, oh,"
thought Dumbo,
"there's going
to be trouble."

And trouble there was!

People began to run away, screaming,
"Wild elephant! Wild elephant!"

The keeper came and put a chain
on Mrs. Jumbo's leg.

He led her away to a small cage.
"Now you won't be able to make
any more trouble," he said.
"Don't take her away,"
cried Dumbo. "It was all my fault."

But the keeper didn't listen.
He shoved Mrs. Jumbo into
the cage and locked the door.
She looked out sadly at her son.
"Be a good little elephant, Dumbo."

The other elephants were upset.
They got together to decide
what to do about Dumbo.

"He can't be part of our act," said one.
"He just makes people laugh."
"Make him a clown, then," said another.

So Dumbo was sent to work with the clowns.
They gave him a ruffled collar.
And they painted his face in a funny way.

This made Dumbo
very sad.
He wanted to be
an elephant—
not a clown.

That evening the elephants performed
without Dumbo.

When they were done, the clowns rushed in
dressed as firemen.

They had a fire engine, a ladder, a hose,
a net, and a tub of water.

But where was Dumbo?

Dumbo was in the burning house.

"Jump, Dumbo, jump!" shouted the clowns.

Even though the flames were not real,

Dumbo was afraid.

But finally Dumbo jumped.
The clowns held tight to the net.
"Hooray!" they shouted.
"You were wonderful!"

But he didn't feel wonderful.
He missed his mother.
And he still didn't want
to be a clown.

The next day Timothy,
the circus mouse, found Dumbo
looking sad.

"Don't be unhappy," he said.
"I will be your friend. I will
find a way to help you.

"Those big ears must be good for something!

"Maybe I can teach
you how to fly with them!"

Timothy took Dumbo to the woods.

There he made a runway out of a log and a board.

"Just flap your ears hard and jump off," he shouted.

Three crows sat on a branch and watched.

Dumbo flapped his ears hard and jumped....

He fell flat on the ground.

"I'll never be able to fly,"
he said.

But clever Timothy had another idea.
He picked up a crow's feather and
handed it to Dumbo. "Take this,"
he said. "It is magic.
Just hold it in
your trunk and jump."

So Dumbo jumped in the air
and flapped his ears.

And all the time he held tight
to the feather.

Suddenly he was flying!

"Good boy, Dumbo!" said Timothy.

The three crows could not believe
their eyes.

Higher and higher he flew.

The green hills and the yellow farm house were far below him.

"Look at him go!" squawked the crow with glasses.

"Now Dumbo will be the star of the circus,"
Timothy said to the crow in the purple hat
and vest.

Dumbo was so happy!

That night Dumbo sat in
the burning house again.

But this time Timothy was riding in his hat.
And in his trunk was the magic feather.
"Jump!" shouted the clowns down below.
"Fly!" whispered Timothy.
Dumbo flew into the air!

But just then
the feather slipped out
of Dumbo's trunk!

"Help! I'm falling! I can't fly without
my feather," cried the little elephant.

Timothy quickly jumped out of the hat
and slid down to Dumbo's trunk.

"Dumbo, Dumbo!" he shouted. "That feather
isn't magic. You can fly without it."

"Really?" asked Dumbo.

"Yes!" said Timothy. "Hurry up!
Flap those ears and FLY!"

The little elephant
began to flap his ears
as fast as he could.

Up, up, up he sailed
to the top of the circus tent.

"I can fly! I can fly!"
cried Dumbo. "Even without
my feather."

"Hooray!" shouted Timothy,
from his seat in Dumbo's hat.
"Now you are a real
circus star! Can you hear
the people cheering?"

The crowd WAS cheering!

"See the amazing flying elephant!" shouted
the ringmaster, as Dumbo flew over his head.

Dumbo made a perfect landing right
in front of the other elephants.
"Well done, Dumbo," they said.

"Dumbo, you were so good," said the ringmaster, "that I will give you anything you want."

Dumbo knew right away what he wanted.

"Please let my mother out of the cage," he said.

The ringmaster agreed
to let Mrs. Jumbo out.
"Do you know your son
is a circus star?" he said to her.
"Are you really?" she asked Dumbo.
"Yes, Mother. I can fly!"
Mrs. Jumbo was so proud of her son.

At last Mrs. Jumbo and her son
were together again.

She patted Dumbo with her trunk.

"I knew you would be
a star someday," she said.

"Yes, but I couldn't have
done it without my friend
Timothy," said Dumbo.

Timothy smiled.
Who could ask for
a better friend than
a flying elephant?

He hoped that he and Dumbo would be
friends for a long time.